Wade's Wiggly Antlers

To Jacob and Nicholas, and all
the adventure lovers in my life — L.B.

For my little brother Jean-Mi, his wife Cathy
and their three beautiful children, Fernanda,
Fernando and Felipe. With all my love — C.B.

Text © 2017 Louise Bradford
Illustrations © 2017 Christine Battuz

Kids Can Press gratefully acknowledges the financial support of the
Government of Ontario, through the Ontario Media Development
Corporation; the Ontario Arts Council; the Canada Council for
the Arts; and the Government of Canada, through the CBF, for our
publishing activity.

Published in Canada and the U.S. by Kids Can Press Ltd.
25 Dockside Drive, Toronto, ON M5A 0B5

Kids Can Press is a Corus Entertainment Inc. company

www.kidscanpress.com

The artwork is this book was rendered by hand-drawing and
digital collage.

Edited by Debbie Rogosin and Jennifer Stokes
Designed by Julia Naimska

Printed and bound in Malaysia in 9/2016 by Tien Wah Press (Pte.) Ltd.

CM 17 0 9 8 7 6 5 4 3 2 1

Library and Archives Canada Cataloguing in Publication

Bradford, Louise, 1966–, author
        Wade's wiggly antlers / written by Louise Bradford;
illustrated by Christine Battuz.

ISBN 978-1-77138-615-9 (hardback)

        I. Battuz, Christine, illustrator II. Title.

PS8603.R3295W34 2017   jC813'.6   C2016-902147-5

Wade's Wiggly Antlers

Written by
Louise Bradford

Illustrated by
Christine Battuz

Kids Can Press

One winter morning, Wade spotted his shadow
on the snow.

"My antlers look like trumpets!" he cheered.
"Doot too da doo!"

His friends all fell in line behind him, tooting
imaginary horns and *rat-a-tat-tat*-ing
make-believe drums.

As the parade zigzagged through the trees,
Wade thought he felt his antlers wiggle.
It's just the wind, he told himself.
Farther along, it seemed like they wiggled again.
It's all this marching, he thought.

But on his way home, with barely a breeze in the air and his footsteps light on the path, it happened again! This time, Wade checked his antlers. They were loose!

Wade ran straight home to show his mother.

"My antlers are wiggly," he cried, as he burst through the door.

Wade's mother gently nudged each one.

"Remember when we talked about your antlers falling off?" she said. "Don't worry. New ones will grow in the summer."

But Wade *was* worried. He would miss his antlers. He used them for so many things ...

paddles for Ping-Pong ...

perches for giving friends rides ...

catcher's mitts for softball ...

and hooks for flying kites!

Wade decided he was
going to keep his antlers.

The next morning, Wade's
wiggly antlers were wobbly.
So instead of playing hockey,
Wade sat on the bench and
kept score. He didn't want
to risk jostling his antlers.

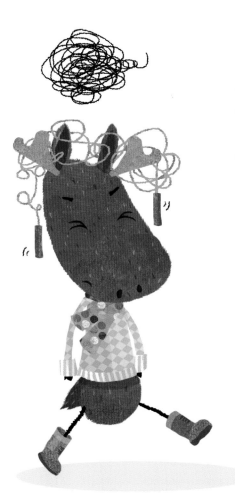

The next day, while his friends played double Dutch, Wade tried to tiptoe in.

After he got untangled, he just turned the rope.

On the third day, while his friends danced, Wade stood alone and softly tapped his hooves to the beat.

Wade was getting tired of being on the sidelines. So on the fourth day, he stayed home.

It was a long day.

That night, Wade couldn't get to sleep. He
kept thinking about all the fun he was missing.
If only he didn't have his antlers to worry about.
    Suddenly, Wade realized it was time for his
antlers to go!

So he gave them a jiggle.

Then he bounced on his bed.

Then he did jumping jacks.
But Wade's antlers didn't budge.

By then, he was sleepy.
I'll try again tomorrow, he thought,
as he snuggled under the covers.

At breakfast, Wade spotted his friends bounding through the forest, pulling a toboggan. Wade loved tobogganing!

"Wait for me!" he hollered, forgetting all about his wobbly antlers.

At the top of the highest hill, Wade and his friends all piled on and down they zoomed.

It was a bumpy ride!

At the bottom, everyone tumbled off and headed back up — everyone except Wade. He stood stock-still. Something was different. He reached up to check his antlers.

They were gone!

Wade peeked at his shadow. *No more trumpets,* he realized a little sadly. *But only for a while,* he reminded himself.

Wade couldn't wait to show his mother. He noticed how much lighter and freer he felt.

This might not be so bad after all, he thought, as he hurried home.

His mother brought out a special box. On the outside, they wrote, "Wade's First Antlers." To celebrate, they made moss cupcakes with maple icing and had a party.
Wade and his friends danced up a storm.

For the rest of the winter and all through the spring, Wade ran faster and jumped higher than he ever had before. He zip-vined through the forest and won at hide-and-seek for the first time.

He hardly missed his antlers at all.

Then one summer morning, as Wade reached up to scratch an itch, he felt two bumps. His new antlers had sprouted!

At first, Wade's antlers didn't look like antlers at all. Instead, they looked like ...

fuzzy acorns ...

then a pair of nut-a-pults ...

then coat hooks.